Simba grew into a happy, healthy cub. One day, he proudly told his uncle, "My dad just showed me the whole kingdom! And I'm going to rule it all."

"He didn't show you what's beyond that rise at the northern border," Scar said slyly. "It's far too dangerous. Only the bravest lions go there. An Elephant Graveyard is no place for a young prince," he added, deliberately tricking his adventurous nephew into exploring that forbidden land.

THE
LION KING

Everything in the animal kingdom had its place in the Circle of Life. When the Lion King, Mufasa, and his queen had a cub named Simba, they knew that one day their son would be king. All the animals bowed in respect as Rafiki the baboon presented the young prince to them.

Only one lion—Mufasa's brother, Scar—refused to attend the ceremony. He was not happy that Simba would be next in line for the throne. *He* wanted to rule the Pride Lands.

Simba raced home and convinced his friend Nala to go to the Elephant Graveyard with him. When they got there, they discovered it was creepier than they had imagined.

Zazu, Mufasa's adviser, caught up with the cubs and warned them to turn back.

But Simba laughed at Zazu. Then he heard someone else laughing. He turned to see three nasty hyenas ready for a meal.

The hyenas cornered the cubs. All of a sudden, there was a tremendous roar. Mufasa had arrived, and he scared away the hyenas.

Mufasa was disappointed that Simba had put himself, Nala, and Zazu in such terrible danger.

That evening, Simba asked his father, "We'll always be together, right?"

"Simba," Mufasa said. "The great kings of the past look down on us from the stars. Remember, those kings will always be there to guide you . . . and so will I."

Meanwhile, Scar made a bargain with the hyenas. If they helped him become king, they could have their run of the Pride Lands. And Scar had a plan—an evil plan.

One day, Scar brought Simba to a gorge and promised him a wonderful surprise if he waited on a certain rock. Then Scar signaled the hyenas to scare a herd of wildebeests, creating a dangerous stampede.

The earth trembled as the wildebeests headed right into the gorge and straight toward Simba. The lion cub jumped up and held on to a tree branch—but he was slipping fast!

In an instant, Mufasa appeared, and helped his son to safety. But then the Lion King slipped off a ledge. He struggled to climb back up, only to find Scar standing above him. Scar knocked his brother off the wall, into the stampede.

When everything was quiet once more, Simba found his father lying lifeless at the bottom of the gorge. Simba had not seen what Scar had done and he believed it was all his own fault.

"Run away, Simba," Scar advised.

Then Scar returned to Pride Rock and announced he would be the new king.

Simba ran and ran until he reached the desert, where he collapsed from exhaustion. Luckily, two curious creatures found him—a meerkat called Timon and a warthog named Pumbaa.

Simba's new friends took him home to the jungle, where they introduced him to *hakuna matata*—a life without worries.

Years passed, and Simba grew up into a young lion. He tried to put the past behind him, but it was difficult.

One day, a young lioness appeared, looking for help. It was his old friend Nala.

"Scar let the hyenas take over the Pride Lands," she explained. "Everything's destroyed. There's no food or water. You must do something or everyone will starve."

Simba could not face going back. But then Rafiki appeared and led him to a vision of his father. "Remember who you are," Mufasa said. "You are my son and the one true king. You must take your place in the Circle of Life."

So Simba returned to the Pride Lands with his friends by his side. There was a great battle. Finally, Scar cornered Simba and confessed what he had done many years earlier. "I killed Mufasa," Scar said coldly.

At last, Simba found the strength to fight back. He knocked the cruel lion right over the edge of the rock into the jaws of the hungry hyenas waiting below.

When the fight was over, Simba took his rightful place as king and restored the Pride Lands to a place of peace.

Months later, Simba and Nala's little cub was born. Rafiki presented the new prince to the kingdom. A brand-new Circle of Life had begun.